CHILDREN'S CLASSICS
EVERYMAN'S LIBRARY

'*They reached the house where the light was burning.*'

Charles Perrault

Little Red Riding Hood and other stories

Translated from the French by
A. E. Johnson
with illustrations by W. Heath Robinson

EVERYMAN'S LIBRARY
CHILDREN'S CLASSICS
Alfred A. Knopf New York Toronto

THIS IS A BORZOI BOOK
PUBLISHED BY ALFRED A. KNOPF, INC.

First included in Everyman's Library 1996
Design and typography © 1996 by David Campbell Publishers Ltd.

Book design by Barbara de Wilde, Carol Devine Carson
and Peter B. Willberg

Five of Ernest H. Shepard's illustrations from *Dream Days* by Kenneth
Grahame are reprinted on the endpapers by permission of The Bodley
Head, London. The sixth illustration is by S. C. Hulme Beaman.

ISBN 0-679-45103-X

Printed and bound in Germany
by Graphischer Grossbetrieb Pössneck GmbH

CONTENTS

LIST OF COLOUR PLATES

THE SLEEPING BEAUTY
IN THE WOOD

O NCE upon a time there lived a king and queen who were grieved, more grieved than words can tell, because they had no children. They tried the waters of every country, made vows and pilgrimages, and did everything that could be done, but without result. At last, however, the queen found that her wishes were fulfilled, and in due course she gave birth to a daughter.

A grand christening was held, and all the fairies that could be found in the realm (they numbered seven in all) were invited to be godmothers to the little princess. This was done so that by means of the gifts which each in turn would bestow upon her (in accordance with the fairy custom of those days) the princess might be endowed with every imaginable perfection.

When the christening ceremony was over, all the company returned to the king's palace, where a great banquet was held in honour of the fairies. Places were laid for them in magnificent style, and before each was placed a solid gold casket containing a spoon, fork, and knife of fine gold, set with diamonds and rubies. But just as all were sitting down to table an aged fairy was seen to enter, whom no one had thought to invite – the reason being that for more than fifty years she had never quitted the tower in which she lived, and people had supposed her to be dead or bewitched.

By the king's orders a place was laid for her, but it was impossible to give her a golden casket like the others, for only seven had been made for the seven fairies. The old creature believed that she was intentionally slighted, and muttered threats between her teeth.

She was overheard by one of the young fairies, who was seated near by. The latter, guessing that some mischievous gift might be bestowed upon the little princess, hid behind the tapestry as soon as the company left the table. Her intention was to be the last to speak, and so to have the power of counteracting, as far as possible, any evil which the old fairy might do.

Presently the fairies began to bestow their gifts upon the princess. The youngest ordained that she should be the most beautiful person in the world; the next, that she should have the temper of an angel; the third, that she should do everything with wonderful grace; the fourth, that she should dance to perfection; the fifth, that she should sing like a nightingale; and the sixth, that she should play every kind of music with the utmost skill.

It was now the turn of the aged fairy. Shaking her head, in token of spite rather than of infirmity, she declared that

'The king . . . at once published an edict'

the princess should prick her hand with a spindle, and die of it. A shudder ran through the company at this terrible gift. All eyes were filled with tears.

But at this moment the young fairy stepped forth from behind the tapestry.

'Take comfort, your Majesties,' she cried in a loud voice; 'your daughter shall not die. My power, it is true, is not enough to undo all that my aged kinswoman has decreed: the princess will indeed prick her hand with a spindle. But instead of dying she shall merely fall into a profound slumber that will last a hundred years. At the end of that time a king's son shall come to awaken her.'

The king, in an attempt to avert the unhappy doom pronounced by the old fairy, at once published an edict forbidding all persons, under pain of death, to use a spinning-wheel or keep a spindle in the house.

At the end of fifteen or sixteen years the king and queen happened one day to be away, on pleasure bent. The princess was running about the castle, and going upstairs from room to room she came at length to a garret at the top of a tower, where an old serving-woman sat alone with her distaff, spinning. This good woman had never heard speak of the king's proclamation forbidding the use of spinning-wheels.

'What are you doing, my good woman?' asked the princess.

13

'I am spinning, my pretty child,' replied the dame, not knowing who she was.

'Oh, what fun!' rejoined the princess; 'how do you do it? Let me try and see if I can do it equally well.'

Partly because she was too hasty, partly because she was a little heedless, but also because the fairy decree had ordained it, no sooner had she seized the spindle than she pricked her hand and fell down in a swoon.

In great alarm the good dame cried out for help. People came running from every quarter to the princess. They threw water on her face, chafed her with their hands, and rubbed her temples with the royal essence of Hungary. But nothing would restore her.

Then the king, who had been brought upstairs by the commotion, remembered the fairy prophecy. Feeling certain that what had happened was inevitable, since the fairies had decreed it, he gave orders that the princess should be placed in the finest apartment in the palace, upon a bed embroidered in gold and silver.

You would have thought her an angel, so fair was she to behold. The trance had not taken away the lovely colour of her complexion. Her cheeks were delicately flushed, her lips like coral. Her eyes, indeed, were closed, but her gentle breathing could be heard, and it was therefore plain that she was not dead. The king commanded that she should be left to sleep in peace until the hour of her awakening should come.

'A little dwarf who had a pair of seven-league boots'

When the accident happened to the princess, the good fairy who had saved her life by condemning her to sleep a hundred years was in the kingdom of Mataquin, twelve thousand leagues away. She was instantly warned of it, however, by a little dwarf who had a pair of seven-league boots, which are boots that enable one to cover seven leagues at a single step. The fairy set off at once, and within an hour her chariot of fire, drawn by dragons, was seen approaching.

The king handed her down from her chariot and she approved of all that he had done. But being gifted with great powers of foresight, she bethought herself that when the princess came to be awakened, she would be much distressed to find herself all alone in the old castle. And this is what she did.

She touched with her wand everybody (except the king and queen) who was in the castle – governesses, maids of honour, ladies-in-waiting, gentlemen, officers, stewards, cooks, scullions, errand boys, guards, porters, pages, footmen. She touched likewise all the horses in the stables, with their grooms, the big mastiffs in the courtyard, and little Puff, the pet dog of the princess, who was lying on the bed beside his mistress. The moment she had touched them they all fell asleep, to awaken only at the same moment as their mistress. Thus they would always be ready with their service whenever she would require it. The very spits before the fire, loaded with partridges and

17

pheasants, subsided into slumber, and the fire as well. All was done in a moment, for the fairies do not take long over their work.

Then the king and queen kissed their dear child, without waking her, and left the castle. Proclamations were issued, forbidding any approach to it, but these warnings were not needed, for within a quarter of an hour there grew up all round the park so vast a quantity of trees big and small, with interlacing brambles and thorns, that neither man nor beast could penetrate them. The tops alone of the castle towers could be seen, and these only from a distance. Thus did the fairy's magic contrive that the princess, during all the time of her slumber, should have nought whatever to fear from prying eyes.

At the end of a hundred years the throne had passed to another family from that of the sleeping princess. One day the king's son chanced to go a-hunting that way, and seeing in the distance some towers in the midst of a large and dense forest, he asked what they were. His attendants told him in reply the various stories which they had heard. Some said there was an old castle haunted by ghosts, others that all the witches of the neighbourhood held their revels there. The favourite tale was that in the castle lived an ogre, who carried thither all the children whom he could catch. There he devoured them at his leisure, and since he was the only person who could force a passage through the wood nobody had been able to pursue him.

'The most beautiful sight he had ever seen'

'The king's son chanced to go a-hunting'

While the prince was wondering what to believe, an old peasant took up the tale.

'Your Highness,' said he, 'more than fifty years ago I heard my father say that in this castle lies a princess, the most beautiful that has ever been seen. It is her doom to sleep there for a hundred years, and then to be awakened by a king's son, for whose coming she waits.'

This story fired the young prince. He jumped immediately to the conclusion that it was for him to see so gay an

21

adventure through, and impelled alike by the wish for love and glory, he resolved to set about it on the spot.

Hardly had he taken a step towards the wood when the tall trees, the brambles and the thorns, separated of themselves and made a path for him. He turned in the direction of the castle, and espied it at the end of a long avenue. This avenue he entered, and was surprised to notice that the

'All asleep'

trees closed up again as soon as he had passed, so that none of his retinue were able to follow him. A young and gallant prince is always brave, however; so he continued on his way, and presently reached a large fore-court.

The sight that now met his gaze was enough to fill him with an icy fear. The silence of the place was dreadful, and death seemed all about him. The recumbent figures of men and animals had all the appearance of being lifeless, until he perceived by the pimply noses and ruddy faces of the porters that they merely slept. It was plain, too, from their glasses, in which were still some dregs of wine, that they had fallen asleep while drinking.

The prince made his way into a great courtyard, paved

22

'They all fell asleep'

with marble, and mounting the staircase entered the guard-room. Here the guards were lined up on either side in two ranks, their muskets on their shoulders, snoring their hardest. Through several apartments crowded with ladies and gentlemen in waiting, some seated, some standing, but all asleep, he pushed on, and so came at last to a chamber which was decked all over with gold. There he encountered the most beautiful sight he had ever seen. Reclining upon a bed, the curtains of which on every side were drawn back, was a princess of seemingly fifteen or sixteen summers, whose radiant beauty had an almost unearthly lustre.

Trembling in his admiration he drew near and went on his knees beside her. At the same moment, the hour of disenchantment having come, the princess awoke, and bestowed upon him a look more tender than a first glance might seem to warrant.

'Is it you, dear prince?' she said; 'you have been long in coming!'

Charmed by these words, and especially by the manner in which they were said, the prince scarcely knew how to express his delight and gratification. He declared that he loved her better than he loved himself. His words were faltering, but they pleased the more for that. The less there is of eloquence, the more there is of love.

Her embarrassment was less than his, and that is not to be wondered at, since she had had time to think of what she would say to him. It seems (although the story says

25

nothing about it) that the good fairy had beguiled her long slumber with pleasant dreams. To be brief, after four hours of talking they had not succeeded in uttering one half of the things they had to say to each other.

Now the whole palace had awakened with the princess. Every one went about his business, and since they were not all in love they presently began to feel mortally hungry. The lady-in-waiting, who was suffering like the rest, at length lost patience, and in a loud voice called out to the princess that supper was served.

The princess was already fully dressed, and in most magnificent style. As he helped her to rise, the prince refrained from telling her that her clothes, with the straight collar which she wore, were like those to which his grand-mother had been accustomed. And in truth, they in no way detracted from her beauty.

They passed into an apartment hung with mirrors, and were there served with supper by the stewards of the house-hold, while the fiddles and oboes played some old music – and played it remarkably well, considering they had not played at all for just upon a hundred years. A little later, when supper was over, the chaplain married them in the castle chapel, and in due course, attended by the courtiers in waiting, they retired to rest.

They slept but little, however. The princess, indeed, had not much need of sleep, and as soon as morning came the prince took his leave of her. He returned to the city, and told his father, who was awaiting him with some anxiety, that he had lost himself while hunting in the forest, but had obtained some black bread and cheese from a charcoal-burner, in whose hovel he had passed the night. His royal father, being of an easy-going nature, believed the tale, but his mother was not so easily hood-winked. She noticed that he now went hunting every day, and that he always had an excuse handy when he had slept two or three nights from home. She felt certain, therefore, that he had some love affair.

Two whole years passed since the marriage of the prince and princess, and during that time they had two children. The first, a daughter, was called 'Dawn,' while the second, a boy, was named 'Day,' because he seemed even more beautiful than his sister.

Many a time the queen told her son that he ought to settle down in life. She tried in this way to make him confide in her, but he did not dare to trust her with his secret. Despite the affection which he bore her, he was afraid of his mother, for she came of a race of ogres, and the king had only married her for her wealth.

It was whispered at the Court that she had ogrish instincts, and that when little children were near her she had the greatest difficulty in the world to keep herself from pouncing on them.

No wonder the prince was reluctant to say a word.

But at the end of two years the king died, and the prince

found himself on the throne. He then made public announcement of his marriage, and went in state to fetch his royal consort from her castle. With her two children beside her she made a triumphal entry into the capital of her husband's realm.

Some time afterwards the king declared war on his neighbour, the Emperor Cantalabutte. He appointed the queen-mother as regent in his absence, and entrusted his wife and children to her care.

He expected to be away at the war for the whole of the summer, and as soon as he was gone the queen-mother sent her daughter-in-law and the two children to a country mansion in the forest. This she did that she might be able the more easily to gratify her horrible longings. A few days later she went there herself, and in the evening summoned the chief steward.

'For my dinner to-morrow,' she told him, 'I will eat little Dawn.'

'Oh, Madam!' exclaimed the steward.

'That is my will,' said the queen; and she spoke in the tones of an ogre who longs for raw meat.

'You will serve her with piquant sauce,' she added.

The poor man, seeing plainly that it was useless to trifle with an ogress, took his knife and went up to little Dawn's chamber. She was at that time four years old, and when she came running with a smile to greet him, flinging her arms round his neck and coaxing him to give her some sweets,

28

he burst into tears, and let the knife fall from his hand.

Presently he went down to the yard behind the house, and slaughtered a young lamb. For this he made so delicious a sauce that his mistress declared she had never eaten anything so good.

At the same time the steward carried little Dawn to his wife, and bade the latter hide her in the quarters which they had below the yard.

Eight days later the wicked queen summoned her steward again.

'For my supper,' she announced, 'I will eat little Day.'

The steward made no answer, being determined to trick her as he had done previously. He went in search of little Day, whom he found with a tiny foil in his hand, making brave passes – though he was but three years old – at a big monkey. He carried him off to his wife, who stowed him away in hiding with little Dawn. To the ogress the steward served up, in place of Day, a young kid so tender that she found it surpassingly delicious.

So far, so good. But there came an evening when this evil queen again addressed the steward.

'I have a mind,' she said, 'to eat the queen with the same sauce as you served with her children.'

This time the poor steward despaired of being able to practise another deception. The young queen was twenty years old, without counting the hundred years she had been asleep. Her skin, though white and beautiful, had become a little tough, and what animal could he possibly find that would correspond to her? He made up his mind that if he would save his own life he must kill the queen, and went upstairs to her apartment determined to do the deed once and for all. Goading himself into a rage he drew the knife and entered the young queen's chamber, but a reluctance to give her no moment of grace made him repeat respectfully the command which he had received from the queen-mother.

'Do it! do it!' she cried, baring her neck to him; 'carry out the order you have been given! Then once more I shall see my children, my poor children that I loved so much!'

Nothing had been said to her when the children were stolen away, and she believed them to be dead.

The poor steward was overcome by compassion. 'No, no, Madam,' he declared; 'you shall not die, but you shall certainly see your children again. That will be in my quarters, where I have hidden them. I shall make the queen eat a young hind in place of you, and thus trick her once more.'

Without more ado he led her to his quarters, and leaving her there to embrace and weep over her children, proceeded to cook a hind with such art that the queen-mother ate it for her supper with as much appetite as if it had indeed been the young queen.

The queen-mother felt well satisfied with her cruel deeds, and planned to tell the king, on his return, that savage wolves had devoured his consort and his children. It was her habit, however, to prowl often about the courts and alleys of the mansion, in the hope of scenting raw meat, and one evening she heard the little boy Day crying in a basement cellar. The child was weeping because his mother had threatened to whip him for some naughtiness, and she heard at the same time the voice of Dawn begging forgiveness for her brother.

The ogress recognised the voices of the queen and her children, and was enraged to find she had been tricked. The next morning, in tones so affrighting that all trembled, she ordered a huge vat to be brought into the middle of the courtyard. This she filled with vipers and toads, with snakes and serpents of every kind, intending to cast into it the queen and her children, and the steward with his wife and serving-girl. By her command these were brought forward, with their hands tied behind their backs.

There they were, and her minions were making ready to cast them into the vat, when into the courtyard rode the king! Nobody had expected him so soon, but he had travelled post-haste. Filled with amazement he demanded to know what this horrible spectacle meant. None dared tell him, and at that moment the ogress, enraged at what confronted her, threw herself head foremost into the vat, and was devoured on the instant by the hideous creatures she had placed in it.

The king could not but be sorry, for after all she was his mother; but it was not long before he found ample consolation in his beautiful wife and children.

PUSS IN BOOTS

A CERTAIN miller had three sons, and when he died the sole worldly goods which he bequeathed to them were his mill, his ass, and his cat. This little legacy was very quickly divided up, and you may be quite sure that neither notary nor attorney were called in to help, for they would speedily have grabbed it all for themselves.

The eldest son took the mill, and the second son took the ass. Consequently all that remained for the youngest son was the cat, and he was not a little disappointed at receiving such a miserable portion.

'My brothers,' said he, 'will be able to get a decent living by joining forces, but for my part, as soon as I have eaten my cat and made a muff out of his skin, I am bound to die of hunger.'

These remarks were overheard by Puss, who pretended not to have been listening, and said very soberly and seriously:

'There is not the least need for you to worry, Master. All you have to do is to give me a pouch, and get a pair of boots made for me so that I can walk in the woods. You will find then that your share is not so bad after all.'

'As though he were dead'

Now this cat had often shown himself capable of per-
forming cunning tricks. When catching rats and mice, for
example, he would hide himself amongst the meal and hang
downwards by the feet as though he were dead. His master,
therefore, though he did not build too much on what the cat
said, felt some hope of being assisted in his miserable plight.

On receiving the boots which he had asked for, Puss gaily
pulled them on. Then he hung the pouch round his neck,
and holding the cords which tied it in front of him with his
paws, he sallied forth to a warren where rabbits abounded.
Placing some bran and lettuce in the pouch, he stretched
himself out and lay as if dead. His plan was to wait until
some young rabbit, unlearned in worldly wisdom, should
come and rummage in the pouch for the eatables which he
had placed there.

Hardly had he laid himself down when things fell out as
he wished. A stupid young rabbit went into the pouch,
and Master Puss, pulling the cords tight, killed him on
the instant.

Well satisfied with his capture, Puss departed to the king's
palace. There he demanded an audience, and was ushered
upstairs. He entered the royal apartment, and bowed pro-
foundly to the king.

'I bring you, Sire,' said he, 'a rabbit from the warren of
the marquis of Carabas (such was the title he invented
for his master), which I am bidden to present to you on
his behalf.'

35

'Tell your master,' replied the king, 'that I thank him, and am pleased by his attention.'

Another time the cat hid himself in a wheatfield, keeping the mouth of his bag wide open. Two partridges ventured in, and by pulling the cords tight he captured both of them. Off he went and presented them to the king, just as he had done with the rabbit from the warren. His Majesty was not less gratified by the brace of partridges, and handed the cat a present for himself.

For two or three months Puss went on in this way, every now and again taking the king, as a present from his master, some game which he had caught. There came a day when he learned that the king intended to take his daughter, who was the most beautiful princess in the world, for an excursion along the river bank.

'If you will do as I tell you,' said Puss to his master, 'your fortune is made. You have only to bathe in the river at the spot which I shall point out to you. Leave the rest to me.'

The marquis of Carabas had no idea what plan was afoot, but did as the cat had directed.

While he was bathing the king drew near, and Puss at once began to cry out at the top of his voice:

'Help! help! the marquis of Carabas is drowning!'

At these shouts the king put his head out of the carriage window. He recognised the cat who had so often brought him game, and bade his escort go speedily to the help of the marquis of Carabas.

'All that remained for the youngest was the cat'

'The cat went on ahead'

While they were pulling the poor marquis out of the river, Puss approached the carriage and explained to the king that while his master was bathing robbers had come and taken away his clothes, though he had cried 'Stop, thief!' at the top of his voice. As a matter of fact, the rascal had hidden them under a big stone. The king at once commanded the keepers of his wardrobe to go and select a suit of his finest clothes for the marquis of Carabas.

The king received the marquis with many compliments, and as the fine clothes which the latter had just put on set

39

off his good looks (for he was handsome and comely in appearance), the king's daughter found him very much to her liking. Indeed, the marquis of Carabas had not bestowed more than two or three respectful but sentimental glances upon her when she fell madly in love with him. The king invited him to enter the coach and join the party.

Delighted to see his plan so successfully launched, the cat went on ahead, and presently came upon some peasants who were mowing a field.

'Listen, my good fellows,' said he; 'if you do not tell the king that the field which you are mowing belongs to the marquis of Carabas, you will all be chopped up into little pieces like mince-meat.'

In due course the king asked the mowers to whom the field on which they were at work belonged.

'It is the property of the marquis of Carabas,' they all cried with one voice, for the threat from Puss had frightened them.

'You have inherited a fine estate,' the king remarked to Carabas.

'As you see for yourself, Sire,' replied the marquis; 'this is a meadow which never fails to yield an abundant crop each year.'

Still travelling ahead, the cat came upon some harvesters.

'Listen, my good fellows,' said he; 'if you do not declare that every one of these fields belongs to the marquis of

Puss in Boots

Carabas, you will all be chopped up into little bits like mince-meat.'

The king came by a moment later, and wished to know who was the owner of the fields in sight.

'It is the marquis of Carabas,' cried the harvesters.

At this the king was more pleased than ever with the marquis.

Preceding the coach on its journey, the cat made the same threat to all whom he met, and the king grew astonished at the great wealth of the marquis of Carabas.

Finally Master Puss reached a splendid castle, which belonged to an ogre. He was the richest ogre that had ever been known, for all the lands through which the king had passed were part of the castle domain.

The cat had taken care to find out who this ogre was, and what powers he possessed. He now asked for an interview, declaring that he was unwilling to pass so close to the castle without having the honour of paying his respects to the owner.

The ogre received him as civilly as an ogre can, and bade him sit down.

'I have been told,' said Puss, 'that you have the power to change yourself into any kind of animal – for example, that you can transform yourself into a lion or an elephant.'

'That is perfectly true,' said the ogre, curtly; 'and just to prove it you shall see me turn into a lion.'

Puss was so frightened on seeing a lion before him that

43

he sprang on to the roof – not without difficulty and danger, for his boots were not meant for walking on the tiles.

Perceiving presently that the ogre had abandoned his transformation, Puss descended, and owned to having been thoroughly frightened.

'I have also been told,' he added, 'but I can scarcely believe it, that you have the further power to take the shape of the smallest animals – for example, that you can change yourself into a rat or a mouse. I confess that to me it seems quite impossible.'

'Impossible?' cried the ogre; 'you shall see!' And in the same moment he changed himself into a mouse, which began to run about the floor. No sooner did Puss see it than he pounced on it and ate it.

Presently the king came along, and noticing the ogre's beautiful mansion desired to visit it. The cat heard the rumble of the coach as it crossed the castle drawbridge, and running out to the courtyard cried to the king:

'Welcome, your Majesty, to the castle of the marquis of Carabas!'

'What's that?' cried the king. 'Is this castle also yours, marquis? Nothing could be finer than this courtyard and buildings which I see all about. With your permission we will go inside and look round.'

The marquis gave his hand to the young princess, and followed the king as he led the way up the staircase. Entering a great hall they found there a magnificent collation.

'Puss became a personage of great importance'

This had been prepared by the ogre for some friends who were to pay him a visit that very day. The latter had not dared to enter when they learned that the king was there.

The king was now quite as charmed with the excellent qualities of the marquis of Carabas as his daughter. The latter was completely captivated by him. Noting the great wealth of which the marquis was evidently possessed, and having quaffed several cups of wine, he turned to his host, saying:

'It rests with you, marquis, whether you will be my son-in-law.'

The marquis, bowing very low, accepted the honour which the king bestowed upon him. The very same day he married the princess.

Puss became a personage of great importance, and gave up hunting mice, except for amusement.

LITTLE TOM THUMB

ONCE upon a time there lived a wood-cutter and his wife, who had seven children, all boys. The eldest was only ten years old, and the youngest was seven. People were astonished that the wood-cutter had had so many children in so short a time, but the reason was that his wife delighted in children, and never had less than two at a time.

They were very poor, and their seven children were a great tax on them, for none of them was yet able to earn his own living. And they were troubled also because the youngest was very delicate and could not speak a word. They mistook for stupidity what was in reality a mark of good sense.

This youngest boy was very little. At his birth he was scarcely bigger than a man's thumb, and he was called in consequence 'Little Tom Thumb.' The poor child was the scapegoat of the family, and got the blame for everything. All the same, he was the sharpest and shrewdest of the brothers, and if he spoke but little he listened much.

There came a very bad year, when the famine was so great that these poor people resolved to get rid of their family. One evening, after the children had gone to bed, the wood-cutter was sitting in the chimney-corner with his wife. His heart was heavy with sorrow as he said to her:

'It must be plain enough to you that we can no longer feed our children. I cannot see them die of hunger before my eyes, and I have made up my mind to take them tomorrow to the forest and lose them there. It will be easy enough to manage, for while they are amusing themselves by collecting faggots we have only to disappear without their seeing us.'

'Ah!' cried the wood-cutter's wife, 'do you mean to say you are capable of letting your own children be lost?'

In vain did her husband remind her of their terrible poverty; she could not agree. She was poor, but she was their mother. In the end, however, reflecting what a grief it would be to see them die of hunger, she consented to the plan, and went weeping to bed.

Little Tom Thumb had heard all that was said. Having discovered, when in bed, that serious talk was going on, he had got up softly, and had slipped under his father's stool in order to listen without being seen. He went back to bed, but did not sleep a wink for the rest of the night, thinking over what he had better do. In the morning he rose very early and went to the edge of a brook. There he filled his pockets with little white pebbles and came quickly home again.

They all set out, and little Tom Thumb said not a word to his brothers of what he knew.

They went into a forest which was so dense that when only ten paces apart they could not see each other. The wood-cutter set about his work, and the children began to collect twigs to make faggots. Presently the father and mother, seeing them busy at their task, edged gradually away, and then hurried off in haste along a little narrow footpath.

When the children found they were alone they began to cry and call out with all their might. Little Tom Thumb let them cry, being confident that they would get back home again. For on the way he had dropped the little white stones which he carried in his pocket all along the path.

'Don't be afraid, brothers,' he said presently; 'our parents have left us here, but I will take you home again. Just follow me.'

They fell in behind him, and he led them straight to their house by the same path which they had taken to the forest. At first they dared not go in, but placed themselves against the door, where they could hear everything their father and mother were saying.

Now the wood-cutter and his wife had no sooner reached home than the lord of the manor sent them a sum of ten crowns which had been owing from him for a long time, and of which they had given up hope. This put new life into them, for the poor creatures were dying of hunger.

'A good dame opened the door'

The wood-cutter sent his wife off to the butcher at once, and as it was such a long time since they had had anything to eat, she bought three times as much meat as a supper for two required.

When they found themselves once more at table, the wood-cutter's wife began to lament.

'Alas! where are our poor children now?' she said; 'they could make a good meal off what we have over. Mind you, William, it was you who wished to lose them: I declared over and over again that we should repent it. What are they doing now in the forest? Merciful heavens, perhaps the wolves have already eaten them! A monster you must be to lose your children in this way!'

At last the wood-cutter lost patience, for she repeated more than twenty times that he would repent it, and that she had told him so. He threatened to beat her if she did not hold her tongue.

It was not that the wood-cutter was less grieved than his wife, but she browbeat him, and he was of the same opinion as many other people, who like a woman to have the knack of saying the right thing, but not the trick of being always in the right.

'Alas!' cried the wood-cutter's wife, bursting into tears, 'where are now my children, my poor children?'

She said it once so loud that the children at the door heard it plainly. Together they all called out:

'Here we are! Here we are!'

She rushed to open the door for them, and exclaimed, as she embraced them:

'How glad I am to see you again, dear children! You must be very tired and very hungry. And you, Peterkin, how muddy you are – come and let me wash you!'

This Peterkin was her eldest son. She loved him more than all the others because he was inclined to be red-headed, and she herself was rather red.

They sat down at the table and ate with an appetite which it did their parents good to see. They all talked at once, as they recounted the fears they had felt in the forest.

The good souls were delighted to have their children with them again, and the pleasure continued as long as the ten crowns lasted. But when the money was all spent they relapsed into their former sadness. They again resolved to lose the children, and to lead them much further away than they had done the first time, so as to do the job thoroughly. But though they were careful not to speak openly about it, their conversation did not escape little Tom Thumb, who made up his mind to get out of the situation as he had done on the former occasion.

But though he got up early to go and collect his little stones, he found the door of the house doubly locked, and he could not carry out his plan.

He could not think what to do until the wood-cutter's wife gave them each a piece of bread for breakfast. Then it occurred to him to use the bread in place of the stones, by throwing crumbs along the path which they took, and he tucked it tight in his pocket.

Their parents led them into the thickest and darkest part of the forest, and as soon as they were there slipped away by a side-path and left them. This did not much trouble little Tom Thumb, for he believed he could easily find the way back by means of the bread which he had scattered wherever he walked. But to his dismay he could not discover a single crumb. The birds had come along and eaten it all.

They were in sore trouble now, for with every step they strayed further, and became more and more entangled in the forest. Night came on and a terrific wind arose, which filled them with dreadful alarm. On every side they seemed to hear nothing but the howling of wolves which were coming to eat them up. They dared not speak or move.

In addition it began to rain so heavily that they were soaked to the skin. At every step they tripped and fell on the wet ground, getting up again covered with mud, not knowing what to do with their hands.

Little Tom Thumb climbed to the top of a tree, in an endeavour to see something. Looking all about him he espied, far away on the other side of the forest, a little light like that of a candle. He got down from the tree, and was terribly disappointed to find that when he was on the ground he could see nothing at all.

After they had walked some distance in the direction of the light, however, he caught a glimpse of it again as they were nearing the edge of the forest. At last they reached the house where the light was burning, but not without much anxiety, for every time they had to go down into a hollow they lost sight of it.

They knocked at the door, and a good dame opened to them. She asked them what they wanted.

Little Tom Thumb explained that they were poor children who had lost their way in the forest, and begged her, for pity's sake, to give them a night's lodging.

Noticing what bonny children they all were, the woman began to cry.

'Alas, my poor little dears!' she said: 'you do not know the place you have come to! Have you not heard that this is the house of an ogre who eats little children?'

'Alas, madam!' answered little Tom Thumb, trembling like all the rest of his brothers, 'what shall we do? One thing is very certain: if you do not take us in, the wolves of the forest will devour us this very night, and that being so we should prefer to be eaten by your husband. Perhaps he may take pity on us, if you plead for us.'

The ogre's wife, thinking she might be able to hide them from her husband till the next morning, allowed them to come in, and put them to warm near a huge fire, where a whole sheep was cooking on the spit for the ogre's supper.

Just as they were beginning to get warm they heard

'He could smell fresh flesh'

two or three great bangs at the door. The ogre had returned. His wife hid them quickly under the bed and ran to open the door.

The first thing the ogre did was to ask whether supper was ready and the wine opened. Then without ado he sat down to table. Blood was still dripping from the sheep, but it seemed all the better to him for that. He sniffed to right and left, declaring that he could smell fresh flesh.

'Indeed!' said his wife. 'It must be the calf which I have just dressed that you smell.'

'*I smell fresh flesh*, I tell you,' shouted the ogre, eyeing his wife askance; 'and there is something going on here which I do not understand.'

With these words he got up from the table and went straight to the bed.

'Aha!' said he; 'so this is the way you deceive me, wicked woman that you are! I have a very great mind to eat you too! It's lucky for you that you are old and tough! I am expecting three ogre friends of mine to pay me a visit in the next few days, and here is a tasty dish which will just come in nicely for them!'

One after another he dragged the children out from under the bed.

The poor things threw themselves on their knees, imploring mercy; but they had to deal with the most cruel of all ogres. Far from pitying them, he was already devouring them with his eyes, and repeating to his wife that when cooked with a good sauce they would make most dainty morsels.

Off he went to get a large knife, which he sharpened, as he drew near the poor children, on a long stone in his left hand.

He had already seized one of them when his wife called out to him. 'What do you want to do it now for?' she said; 'will it not be time enough tomorrow?'

'Hold your tongue,' replied the ogre; 'they will be all the more tender.'

'But you have such a lot of meat,' rejoined his wife; 'look, there are a calf, two sheep, and half a pig.'

'You are right,' said the ogre; 'give them a good supper to fatten them up, and take them to bed.'

The good woman was overjoyed and brought them a splendid supper; but the poor little wretches were so cowed with fright that they could not eat.

As for the ogre, he went back to his drinking, very pleased to have such good entertainment for his friends. He drank a dozen cups more than usual, and was obliged to go off to bed early, for the wine had gone somewhat to his head.

Now the ogre had seven daughters who as yet were only children. These little ogresses all had the most lovely complexions, for, like their father, they ate fresh meat. But they had little round grey eyes, crooked noses, and very large mouths, with long and exceedingly sharp teeth, set far

'He set off over the countryside'

apart. They were not so very wicked at present, but they showed great promise, for already they were in the habit of killing little children to suck their blood.

They had gone to bed early, and were all seven in a great bed, each with a crown of gold upon her head.

In the same room there was another bed, equally large, Into this the ogre's wife put the seven little boys, and then went to sleep herself beside her husband.

Little Tom Thumb was fearful lest the ogre should suddenly regret that he had not cut the throats of himself and his brothers the evening before. Having noticed that the ogre's daughters all had golden crowns upon their heads, he got up in the middle of the night and softly placed his own cap and those of his brothers on their heads. Before doing so, he carefully removed the crowns of gold, putting them on his own and his brothers' heads. In this way, if the ogre were to feel like slaughtering them that night he would mistake the girls for the boys, and *vice versa*.

Things fell out just as he had anticipated. The ogre, waking up at midnight, regretted that he had postponed till the morrow what he could have done overnight. Jumping briskly out of bed, he seized his knife, crying: 'Now then, let's see how the little rascals are; we won't make the same mistake twice!'

He groped his way up to his daughters' room, and approached the bed in which were the seven little boys. All were sleeping, with the exception of little Tom Thumb, who was numb with fear when he felt the ogre's hand, as it touched the head of each brother in turn, reach his own.

'Upon my word,' said the ogre, as he felt the golden crowns; 'a nice job I was going to make of it! It is very evident that I drank a little too much last night!'

Forthwith he went to the bed where his daughters were, and here he felt the little boys' caps.

'Aha, here are the little scamps!' he cried; 'now for a smart bit of work!'

With these words, and without a moment's hesitation, he cut the throats of his seven daughters, and well satisfied with his work went back to bed beside his wife.

No sooner did little Tom Thumb hear him snoring than he woke up his brothers, bidding them dress quickly and follow him. They crept quietly down to the garden, and jumped from the wall. All through the night they ran in haste and terror, without the least idea of where they were going.

When the ogre woke up he said to his wife:

'Go upstairs and dress those little rascals who were here last night.'

The ogre's wife was astonished at her husband's kindness, never doubting that he meant her to go and put on their clothes. She went upstairs, and was horrified to discover her seven daughters bathed in blood, with their throats cut.

She fell at once into a swoon, which is the way of most women in similar circumstances.

The ogre, thinking his wife was very long in carrying out his orders, went up to help her, and was no less astounded than his wife at the terrible spectacle which confronted him.

'What's this I have done?' he exclaimed. 'I will be revenged on the wretches, and quickly, too!'

He threw a jugful of water over his wife's face, and having brought her round ordered her to fetch his seven-league boots, so that he might overtake the children.

He set off over the countryside, and strode far and wide until he came to the road along which the poor children were travelling. They were not more than a few yards from their home when they saw the ogre striding from hill-top to hill-top, and stepping over rivers as though they were merely tiny streams.

Little Tom Thumb espied near at hand a cave in some rocks. In this he hid his brothers, and himself followed them in, while continuing to keep a watchful eye upon the movements of the ogre.

Now the ogre was feeling very tired after so much fruitless marching (for seven-league boots are very fatiguing to their wearer), and felt like taking a little rest. As it happened, he went and sat down on the very rock beneath which the little boys were hiding. Overcome with weariness, he had not sat there long before he fell asleep and began to snore so terribly that the poor children were as frightened as when he had held his great knife to their throats.

Little Tom Thumb was not so alarmed. He told his brothers to flee at once to their home while the ogre was still sleeping soundly, and not to worry about him. They took his advice and ran quickly home.

Little Tom Thumb now approached the ogre and gently pulled off his boots, which he at once donned himself. The boots were very heavy and very large, but being enchanted boots they had the faculty of growing larger or smaller according to the leg they had to suit. Consequently they always fitted as though they had been made for the wearer.

He went straight to the ogre's house, where he found the ogre's wife weeping over her murdered daughters.

'Your husband,' said little Tom Thumb, 'is in great danger, for he has been captured by a gang of thieves, and the latter have sworn to kill him if he does not hand over all his gold and silver. Just as they had the dagger at his throat, he caught sight of me and begged me to come to you and thus rescue him from his terrible plight. You are to give me everything of value which he possesses, without keeping back a thing, otherwise he will be slain without mercy. As the matter is urgent he wished me to wear his seven-league boots, to save time, and also to prove to you that I am no impostor.'

'Laden with all the ogre's wealth'

The ogre's wife, in great alarm, gave him immediately all that she had, for although this was an ogre who devoured little children, he was by no means a bad husband.

Little Tom Thumb, laden with all the ogre's wealth, forthwith repaired to his father's house, where he was received with great joy.

Many people do not agree about this last adventure, and pretend that little Tom Thumb never committed this theft from the ogre, and only took the seven-league boots, about which he had no compunction, since they were only used by the ogre for catching little children. These folks assert that they are in a position to know, having been guests at the wood-cutter's cottage. They further say that when little Tom Thumb had put on the ogre's boots, he went off to the Court, where he knew there was great anxiety concerning the result of a battle which was being fought by an army two hundred leagues away.

They say that he went to the king and undertook, if desired, to bring news of the army before the day was out; and that the king promised him a large sum of money if he could carry out his project.

Little Tom Thumb brought news that very night, and this first errand having brought him into notice, he made as much money as he wished. For not only did the king pay him handsomely to carry orders to the army, but many ladies at the court gave him anything he asked to get them news of their lovers, and this was his greatest source of income. He was occasionally entrusted by wives with letters to their husbands, but they paid him so badly, and this branch of the business brought him in so little, that he did not even bother to reckon what he made from it.

After acting as courier for some time, and amassing great wealth thereby, little Tom Thumb returned to his father's house, and was there greeted with the greatest joy imaginable. He made all his family comfortable, buying newly-created positions for his father and brothers. In this way he set them all up, not forgetting at the same time to look well after himself.

THE FAIRIES

ONCE upon a time there lived a widow with two daughters. The elder was often mistaken for her mother, so like her was she both in nature and in looks; parent and child being so disagreeable and arrogant that no one could live with them.

The younger girl, who took after her father in the gentleness and sweetness of her disposition, was also one of the prettiest girls imaginable. The mother doted on the elder daughter – naturally enough, since she resembled her so closely – and disliked the younger one as intensely. She made the latter live in the kitchen and work hard from morning till night.

One of the poor child's many duties was to go twice a day and draw water from a spring a good half-mile away, bringing it back in a large pitcher. One day when she was at the spring an old woman came up and begged for a drink.

'Why, certainly, good mother,' the pretty lass replied. Rinsing her pitcher, she drew some water from the cleanest part of the spring and handed it to the dame, lifting up the jug so that she might drink the more easily.

Now this old woman was a fairy, who had taken the form of a poor village dame to see just how far the girl's good nature would go. 'You are so pretty,' she said, when she had finished drinking, 'and so polite, that I am determined to bestow a gift upon you. This is the boon I grant you: with every word that you utter there shall fall from your mouth either a flower or a precious stone.'

When the girl reached home she was scolded by her mother for being so long in coming back from the spring.

'I am sorry to have been so long, mother,' said the poor child.

As she spoke these words there fell from her mouth three roses, three pearls, and three diamonds.

'What's this?' cried her mother; 'did I see pearls and diamonds dropping out of your mouth? What does this mean, dear daughter?' (This was the first time she had ever addressed her daughter affectionately.)

The poor child told a simple tale of what had happened, and in speaking scattered diamonds right and left.

'Really,' said her mother, 'I must send my own child there. Come here, Fanchon; look what comes out of your sister's mouth whenever she speaks! Wouldn't you like to be able to do the same? All you have to do is to go and draw some water at the spring, and when a poor woman asks you for a drink, give it her very nicely.'

'Oh, indeed!' replied the ill-mannered girl; 'don't you wish you may see me going there!'

'Lifting up the jug so that she might drink the more easily'

'I tell you that you are to go,' said her mother, 'and to go this instant.'

Very sulkily the girl went off, taking with her the best silver flagon in the house. No sooner had she reached the spring than she saw a lady, magnificently attired, who came towards her from the forest, and asked for a drink. This was the same fairy who had appeared to her sister, masquerading now as a princess in order to see how far this girl's ill-nature would carry her.

'Do you think I have come here just to get you a drink?' said the loutish damsel, arrogantly. 'I suppose you think I brought a silver flagon here specially for that purpose – it's so likely, isn't it? Drink from the spring, if you want to!'

'You are not very polite,' said the fairy, displaying no sign of anger. 'Well, in return for your lack of courtesy I decree that for every word you utter a snake or a toad shall drop out of your mouth.'

The moment her mother caught sight of her coming back she cried out, 'Well, daughter?'

'Well, mother?' replied the rude girl. As she spoke a viper and a toad were spat out of her mouth.

'Gracious heavens!' cried her mother; 'what do I see? Her sister is the cause of this, and I will make her pay for it!'

Off she ran to thrash the poor child, but the latter fled away and hid in the forest near by. The king's son met her on his way home from hunting, and noticing how pretty she was inquired what she was doing all alone, and what she was weeping about.

'Alas, sir,' she cried; 'my mother has driven me from home!'

As she spoke the prince saw four or five pearls and as many diamonds fall from her mouth. He begged her to tell him how this came about, and she told him the whole story.

The king's son fell in love with her, and reflecting that such a gift as had been bestowed upon her was worth more than any dowry which another maiden might bring him, he took her to the palace of his royal father, and there married her.

As for the sister, she made herself so hateful that even her mother drove her out of the house. Nowhere could the wretched girl find any one who would take her in, and at last she lay down in the forest and died.

RICKY OF THE TUFT

O NCE upon a time there was a queen who bore a son so ugly and misshapen that for some time it was doubtful if he would have human form at all. But a fairy who was present at his birth promised that he should have plenty of brains, and added that by virtue of the gift which she had just bestowed upon him he would be able to impart to the person whom he should love best the same degree of intelligence which he possessed himself.

This somewhat consoled the poor queen, who was greatly disappointed at having brought into the world such a hideous brat. And indeed, no sooner did the child begin to speak than his sayings proved to be full of shrewdness, while all that he did was somehow so clever that he charmed every one.

I forgot to mention that when he was born he had a little tuft of hair upon his head. For this reason he was called Ricky of the Tuft, Ricky being his family name.

Some seven or eight years later the queen of a neighbouring kingdom gave birth to twin daughters. The first one to come into the world was more beautiful than the dawn, and the queen was so overjoyed that it was feared her great excitement might do her some harm. The same fairy who had assisted at the birth of Ricky of the Tuft was present, and, in order to moderate the transports of the queen she declared that this little princess would have no sense at all, and would be as stupid as she was beautiful.

The queen was deeply mortified, and a moment or two later her chagrin became greater still, for the second daughter proved to be extremely ugly.

'Do not be distressed, Madam,' said the fairy; 'your daughter shall be recompensed in another way. She shall have so much good sense that her lack of beauty will scarcely be noticed.'

'May Heaven grant it!' said the queen; 'but is there no means by which the elder, who is so beautiful, can be endowed with some intelligence?'

'In the matter of brains I can do nothing for her, Madam,' said the fairy, 'but as regards beauty I can do a great deal. As there is nothing I would not do to please you, I will bestow upon her the power of making beautiful any person who shall greatly please her.'

As the two princesses grew up their perfections increased, and everywhere the beauty of the elder and the wit of the younger were the subject of common talk.

It is equally true that their defects also increased as they became older. The younger grew uglier every minute, and the elder daily became more stupid. Either she answered nothing at all when spoken to, or replied with some idiotic

78

'She could not set four china vases on the mantelpiece without breaking one of them'

remark. At the same time she was so awkward that she could not set four china vases on the mantelpiece without breaking one of them, nor drink a glass of water without spilling half of it over her clothes.

'Graceful and easy conversation'

Now although the elder girl possessed the great advantage which beauty always confers upon youth, she was nevertheless outshone in almost all company by her younger sister. At first every one gathered round the beauty to see and admire her, but very soon they were all attracted by the graceful and easy conversation of the clever one. In a very short time the elder girl would be left entirely alone, while everybody clustered round her sister.

The elder princess was not so stupid that she was not aware of this, and she would willingly have surrendered all her beauty for half her sister's cleverness. Sometimes she was ready to die of grief, for the queen, though a sensible woman, could not refrain from occasionally reproaching her with her stupidity.

The princess had retired one day to a wood to bemoan her misfortune, when she saw approaching her an ugly little man, of very disagreeable appearance, but clad in magnificent attire.

This was the young prince Ricky of the Tuft. He had fallen in love with her portrait, which was everywhere to be seen, and had left his father's kingdom in order to have the pleasure of seeing and talking to her.

Delighted to meet her thus alone, he approached with every mark of respect and politeness. But while he paid her the usual compliments he noticed that she was plunged in melancholy.

'I cannot understand, madam,' he said, 'how any one with your beauty can be so sad as you appear. I can boast of having seen many fair ladies, and I declare that none of them could compare in beauty with you.'

'It is very kind of you to say so, sir,' answered the princess; and stopped there, at a loss what to say further.

'Beauty,' said Ricky, 'is of such great advantage that

everything else can be disregarded; and I do not see that the possessor of it can have anything much to grieve about.'

To this the princess replied:

'I would rather be as plain as you are and have some sense, than be as beautiful as I am and at the same time stupid.'

'Nothing more clearly displays good sense, madam, than a belief that one is not possessed of it. It follows, therefore, that the more one has, the more one fears it to be wanting.'

'I am not sure about that,' said the princess; 'but I know only too well that I am very stupid, and this is the reason of the misery which is nearly killing me.'

'If that is all that troubles you, madam, I can easily put an end to your suffering.'

'How will you manage that?' said the princess.

'I am able, madam,' said Ricky of the Tuft, 'to bestow as much good sense as it is possible to possess on the person whom I love the most. You are that person, and it therefore rests with you to decide whether you will acquire so much intelligence. The only condition is that you shall consent to marry me.'

The princess was dumbfounded, and remained silent.

'I can see,' pursued Ricky, 'that this suggestion perplexes you, and I am not surprised. But I will give you a whole year to make up your mind to it.'

The princess had so little sense, and at the same time

desired it so ardently, that she persuaded herself the end of this year would never come. So she accepted the offer which had been made to her. No sooner had she given her word to Ricky that she would marry him within one year from that very day, than she felt a complete change come over her. She found herself able to say all that she wished with the greatest ease, and to say it in an elegant, finished, and natural manner. She at once engaged Ricky in a brilliant and lengthy conversation, holding her own so well that Ricky feared he had given her a larger share of sense than he had retained for himself.

On her return to the palace amazement reigned throughout the Court at such a sudden and extraordinary change. Whereas formerly they had been accustomed to hear her give vent to silly, pert remarks, they now heard her express herself sensibly and very wittily.

The entire Court was overjoyed. The only person not too pleased was the younger sister, for now that she had no longer the advantage over the elder in wit, she seemed nothing but a little fright in comparison.

The king himself often took her advice, and several times held his councils in her apartment.

The news of this change spread abroad, and the princes of the neighbouring kingdoms made many attempts to captivate her. Almost all asked her in marriage. But she found none with enough sense, and so she listened to all without promising herself to any.

At last came one who was so powerful, so rich, so witty, and so handsome, that she could not help being somewhat attracted by him. Her father noticed this, and told her she could make her own choice of a husband: she had only to declare herself.

Now the more sense one has, the more difficult it is to make up one's mind in an affair of this kind. After thanking her father, therefore, she asked for a little time to think it over.

In order to ponder quietly what she had better do she went to walk in a wood – the very one, as it happened, where she encountered Ricky of the Tuft.

While she walked, deep in thought, she heard beneath her feet a thudding sound, as though many people were running busily to and fro. Listening more attentively she heard voices. 'Bring me that boiler,' said one; then another – 'Put some wood on that fire!'

At that moment the ground opened, and she saw below what appeared to be a large kitchen full of cooks and scullions, and all the train of attendants which the preparation of a great banquet involves. A gang of some twenty or thirty spit-turners emerged and took up their positions round a very long table in a path in the wood. They all wore their cook's caps on one side, and with their basting implements in their hands they kept time together as they worked, to the lilt of a melodious song.

The princess was astonished by this spectacle, and asked for whom their work was being done.

85

'For Prince Ricky of the Tuft, madam,' said the foreman of the gang; 'his wedding is tomorrow.'

At this the princess was more surprised than ever. In a flash she remembered that it was a year to the very day since she had promised to marry Prince Ricky of the Tuft, and was taken aback by the recollection. The reason she had forgotten was that when she made the promise she was still without sense, and with the acquisition of that intelligence which the prince had bestowed upon her, all memory of her former stupidities had been blotted out.

She had not gone another thirty paces when Ricky of the Tuft appeared before her, gallant and resplendent, like a prince upon his wedding day.

'As you see, madam,' he said, 'I keep my word to the minute. I do not doubt that you have come to keep yours, and by giving me your hand to make me the happiest of men.'

'I will be frank with you,' replied the princess. 'I have not yet made up my mind on the point, and I am afraid I shall never be able to take the decision you desire.'

'You astonish me, madam,' said Ricky of the Tuft.

'I can well believe it,' said the princess, 'and undoubtedly, if I had to deal with a clown, or a man who lacked good sense, I should feel myself very awkwardly situated. "A princess must keep her word," he would say, "and you must marry me because you promised to!" But I am speaking to a man of the world, of the greatest good sense,

Ricky of the Tuft

and I am sure that he will listen to reason. As you are aware, I could not make up my mind to marry you even when I was entirely without sense; how can you expect that to-day, possessing the intelligence you bestowed on me, which makes me still more difficult to please than formerly, I should take a decision which I could not take then? If you wished so much to marry me, you were very wrong to relieve me of my stupidity, and to let me see more clearly than I did.'

'If a man who lacked good sense,' replied Ricky of the Tuft, 'would be justified, as you have just said, in reproaching you for breaking your word, why do you expect, madam, that I should act differently where the happiness of my whole life is at stake? Is it reasonable that people who have sense should be treated worse than those who have none? Would you maintain that for a moment – you, who so markedly have sense, and desired so ardently to have it? But, pardon me, let us get to the facts. With the exception of my ugliness, is there anything about me which displeases you? Are you dissatisfied with my breeding, my brains, my disposition, or my manners?'

'In no way,' replied the princess; 'I like exceedingly all that you have displayed of the qualities you mention.'

'In that case,' said Ricky of the Tuft, 'happiness will be mine, for it lies in your power to make me the most attractive of men.'

'How can that be done?' asked the princess.

'It will happen of itself,' replied Ricky of the Tuft, 'if you love me well enough to wish that it be so. To remove your doubts, madam, let me tell you that the same fairy who on the day of my birth bestowed upon me the power of endowing with intelligence the woman of my choice, gave to you also the power of endowing with beauty the man whom you should love, and on whom you should wish to confer this favour.'

'If that is so,' said the princess, 'I wish with all my heart that you may become the handsomest and most attractive prince in the world, and I give you without reserve the boon which it is mine to bestow.'

No sooner had the princess uttered these words than Ricky of the Tuft appeared before her eyes as the handsomest, most graceful and attractive man that she had ever set eyes on.

Some people assert that this was not the work of fairy enchantment, but that love alone brought about the transformation. They say that the princess, as she mused upon her lover's constancy, upon his good sense, and his many admirable qualities of heart and head, grew blind to the deformity of his body and the ugliness of his face; that his hump back seemed no more than was natural in a man who could make the courtliest of bows, and that the dreadful limp which had formerly distressed her now betokened nothing more than a certain diffidence and charming deference of manner. They say further that she found his eyes shine all the brighter for their squint, and that this defect in them was to her but a sign of passionate love; while his great red nose she found nought but martial and heroic.

However that may be, the princess promised to marry him on the spot, provided only that he could obtain the consent of her royal father.

The king knew Ricky of the Tuft to be a prince both wise and witty, and on learning of his daughter's regard for him, accepted him with pleasure as a son-in-law.

The wedding took place upon the morrow, just as Ricky of the Tuft had foreseen, and in accordance with the arrangements he had long ago put in train.

CINDERELLA

O NCE upon a time there was a worthy man who married for his second wife the haughtiest, proudest woman that had ever been seen. She had two daughters, who possessed their mother's temper and resembled her in everything. Her husband, on the other hand, had a young daughter, who was of an exceptionally sweet and gentle nature. She got this from her mother, who had been the nicest person in the world.

The wedding was no sooner over than the stepmother began to display her bad temper. She could not endure the excellent qualities of this young girl, for they made her own daughters appear more hateful than ever. She thrust upon her all the meanest tasks about the house. It was she who had to clean the plates and the stairs, and sweep out the rooms of the mistress of the house and her daughters. She slept on a wretched mattress in a garret at the top of the house, while the sisters had rooms with parquet flooring, and beds of the fashionable style, with mirrors in which they could see themselves from top to toe.

The poor girl endured everything patiently, not daring to complain to her father. The latter would have scolded

92

'The haughtiest, proudest woman that had ever been seen'

her, because he was entirely ruled by his wife. When she had finished her work she used to sit amongst the cinders in the corner of the chimney, and it was from this habit that she came to be commonly known as Cinder-slut. The younger of the two sisters, who was not quite so spiteful as the elder, called her Cinderella. But her wretched clothes did not prevent Cinderella from being a hundred times more beautiful than her sisters, for all their resplendent garments.

It happened that the king's son gave a ball, and he invited all persons of high degree. The two young ladies were invited amongst others, for they cut a considerable figure in the country. Not a little pleased were they, and the question of what clothes and what mode of dressing the hair would become them best took up all their time. And all this meant fresh trouble for Cinderella, for it was she who went over her sisters' linen and ironed their ruffles. They could talk of nothing else but the fashions in clothes.

'For my part,' said the elder, 'I shall wear my dress of red velvet, with the Honiton lace.'

'I have only my everyday petticoat,' said the younger, 'but to make up for it I shall wear my cloak with the golden flowers and my necklace of diamonds, which are not so bad.'

They sent for a good hairdresser to arrange their double-frilled caps, and bought patches at the best shop.

They summoned Cinderella and asked her advice, for

she had good taste. Cinderella gave them the best possible suggestions, and even offered to dress their hair, to which they gladly agreed.

While she was thus occupied they said:

'Cinderella, would you like to go to the ball?'

'Ah, but you fine young ladies are laughing at me. It would be no place for me.'

'That is very true, people would laugh to see a cinder-slut in the ballroom.'

Any one else but Cinderella would have done their hair amiss, but she was good-natured, and she finished them off to perfection. They were so excited in their glee that for nearly two days they ate nothing. They broke more than a dozen laces through drawing their stays tight in order to make their waists more slender, and they were perpetually in front of a mirror.

At last the happy day arrived. Away they went, Cinderella watching them as long as she could keep them in sight. When she could no longer see them she began to cry. Her godmother found her in tears, and asked what was troubling her.

'I should like – I should like –'

She was crying so bitterly that she could not finish the sentence.

Said her godmother, who was a fairy:

'You would like to go to the ball, would you not?'

'Ah, yes,' said Cinderella, sighing.

'Her godmother found her in tears'

'Well, well,' said her godmother, 'promise to be a good girl and I will arrange for you to go.'

She took Cinderella into her room and said:

'Go into the garden and bring me a pumpkin.'

Cinderella went at once and gathered the finest that she could find. This she brought to her godmother, wondering how a pumpkin could help in taking her to the ball.

Her godmother scooped it out, and when only the rind was left, struck it with her wand. Instantly the pumpkin was changed into a beautiful coach, gilded all over.

Then she went and looked in the mouse-trap, where she found six mice all alive. She told Cinderella to lift the door of the mouse-trap a little, and as each mouse came out she gave it a tap with her wand, whereupon it was transformed into a fine horse. So that here was a fine team of six dappled mouse-grey horses.

But she was puzzled to know how to provide a coachman.

'I will go and see,' said Cinderella, 'if there is not a rat in the rat-trap. We could make a coachman of him.'

'Quite right,' said her godmother, 'go and see.'

Cinderella brought in the rat-trap, which contained three big rats. The fairy chose one specially on account of his elegant whiskers.

As soon as she had touched him he turned into a fat coachman with the finest moustachios that ever were seen.

'Now go into the garden and bring me the six lizards which you will find behind the water-butt.'

No sooner had they been brought than the godmother turned them into six lackeys, who at once climbed up behind the coach in their braided liveries, and hung on there as if they had never done anything else all their lives.

Then said the fairy godmother:

'Well, there you have the means of going to the ball. Are you satisfied?'

'Oh, yes, but am I to go like this in my ugly clothes?'

Her godmother merely touched her with her wand, and on the instant her clothes were changed into garments of gold and silver cloth, bedecked with jewels. After that her godmother gave her a pair of glass slippers, the prettiest in the world.

Thus altered, she entered the coach. Her godmother bade her not to stay beyond midnight whatever happened, warning her that if she remained at the ball a moment longer, her coach would again become a pumpkin, her horses mice, and her lackeys lizards, while her old clothes would reappear upon her once more.

She promised her godmother that she would not fail to leave the ball before midnight, and away she went, beside herself with delight.

The king's son, when he was told of the arrival of a great princess whom nobody knew, went forth to receive her. He handed her down from the coach, and led her into the hall where the company was assembled. At once there fell a great silence. The dancers stopped, the violins played no more, so rapt was the attention which everybody bestowed upon the superb beauty of the unknown guest. Everywhere could be heard in confused whispers:

'Oh, how beautiful she is!'

The king, old man as he was, could not take his eyes off her, and whispered to the queen that it was many a long day since he had seen any one so beautiful and charming.

'Away she went'

All the ladies were eager to scrutinise her clothes and the dressing of her hair, being determined to copy them on the morrow, provided they could find materials so fine, and tailors so clever.

The king's son placed her in the seat of honour, and at once begged the privilege of being her partner in a dance. Such was the grace with which she danced that the admiration of all was increased.

A magnificent supper was served, but the young prince could eat nothing, so taken up was he with watching her. She went and sat beside her sisters, and bestowed numberless attentions upon them. She made them share with her the oranges and lemons which the king had given her – greatly to their astonishment, for they did not recognise her.

While they were talking, Cinderella heard the clock strike a quarter to twelve. She at once made a profound curtsey to the company, and departed as quickly as she could.

As soon as she was home again she sought out her god-mother, and having thanked her, declared that she wished to go upon the morrow once more to the ball, because the king's son had invited her.

While she was busy telling her godmother all that had happened at the ball, her two sisters knocked at the door. Cinderella let them in.

'What a long time you have been in coming!' she declared, rubbing her eyes and stretching herself as if she had only just awakened. In real truth she had not for a moment wished to sleep since they had left.

'If you had been at the ball,' said one of the sisters, 'you would not be feeling weary. There came a most beautiful princess, the most beautiful that has ever been seen, and she bestowed numberless attentions upon us, and gave us her oranges and lemons.'

Cinderella was overjoyed. She asked them the name of the princess, but they replied that no one knew it, and that the king's son was so distressed that he would give anything in the world to know who she was.

'She rose and fled as nimbly as a fawn'

Cinderella smiled, and said she must have been beautiful indeed.

'Oh, how lucky you are. Could I not manage to see her? Oh, please, Javotte, lend me the yellow dress which you wear every day.'

'Indeed!' said Javotte, 'that is a fine idea. Lend my dress to a grubby cinder-slut like you – you must think me mad!'

Cinderella had expected this refusal. She was in no way upset, for she would have been very greatly embarrassed had her sister been willing to lend the dress.

The next day the two sisters went to the ball, and so did Cinderella, even more splendidly attired than the first time.

The king's son was always at her elbow, and paid her endless compliments.

The young girl enjoyed herself so much that she forgot her godmother's bidding completely, and when the first stroke of midnight fell upon her ears, she thought it was no more than eleven o'clock.

She rose and fled as nimbly as a fawn. The prince followed her, but could not catch her. She let fall one of her glass slippers, however, and this the prince picked up with tender care.

When Cinderella reached home she was out of breath, without coach, without lackeys, and in her shabby clothes. Nothing remained of all her splendid clothes save one of the little slippers, the fellow to the one which she had let fall.

Inquiries were made of the palace doorkeepers as to whether they had seen a princess go out, but they declared they had seen no one leave except a young girl, very ill-clad, who looked more like a peasant than a young lady.

When her two sisters returned from the ball, Cinderella asked them if they had again enjoyed themselves, and if the beautiful lady had been there. They told her that she was present, but had fled away when midnight sounded, and in such haste that she had let fall one of her little glass slippers, the prettiest thing in the world. They added that the king's son, who picked it up, had done nothing but gaze at it for the rest of the ball, from which it was plain that he was deeply in love with its beautiful owner.

They spoke the truth. A few days later, the king's son caused a proclamation to be made by trumpeters, that he would take for wife the owner of the foot which the slipper would fit.

They tried it first on the princesses, then on the duchesses and the whole Court, but in vain. Presently they brought it to the home of the two sisters, who did all they could to squeeze a foot into the slipper. This, however, they could not manage.

Cinderella was looking on and recognised her slipper:

'Let me see,' she cried, laughingly, 'if it will not fit me.'

Her sisters burst out laughing, and began to gibe at her, but the equerry who was trying on the slipper looked closely at Cinderella. Observing that she was very beautiful he

'They tried it first on the princesses'

declared that the claim was quite a fair one, and that his orders were to try the slipper on every maiden. He bade Cinderella sit down, and on putting the slipper to her little foot he perceived that the latter slid in without trouble, and was moulded to its shape like wax.

Great was the astonishment of the two sisters at this, and greater still when Cinderella drew from her pocket the other little slipper. This she likewise drew on.

At that very moment her godmother appeared on the scene. She gave a tap with her wand to Cinderella's clothes, and transformed them into a dress even more magnificent than her previous ones.

The two sisters recognised her for the beautiful person whom they had seen at the ball, and threw themselves at her feet, begging her pardon for all the ill-treatment she had suffered at their hands.

Cinderella raised them, and declaring as she embraced them that she pardoned them with all her heart, bade them to love her well in future.

She was taken to the palace of the young prince in all her new array. He found her more beautiful than ever, and was married to her a few days afterwards.

Cinderella was as good as she was beautiful. She set aside apartments in the palace for her two sisters, and married them the very same day to two gentlemen of high rank about the Court.

LITTLE RED RIDING HOOD

ONCE upon a time there was a little village girl, the prettiest that had ever been seen. Her mother doted on her. Her grandmother was even fonder, and made her a little red hood, which became her so well that everywhere she went by the name of Little Red Riding Hood.

One day her mother, who had just made and baked some cakes, said to her:

'Go and see how your grandmother is, for I have been told that she is ill. Take her a cake and this little pot of butter.'

Little Red Riding Hood set off at once for the house of her grandmother, who lived in another village.

On her way through a wood she met old Father Wolf. He would have very much liked to eat her, but dared not do so on account of some wood-cutters who were in the forest. He asked her where she was going. The poor child, not knowing that it was dangerous to stop and listen to a wolf, said:

'I am going to see my grandmother, and am taking her a cake and a pot of butter which my mother has sent to her.'

Little Red Riding Hood

'Does she live far away?' asked the Wolf.

'Oh yes,' replied Little Red Riding Hood; 'it is yonder by the mill which you can see right below there, and it is the first house in the village.'

'She met old Father Wolf'

'Well now,' said the Wolf, 'I think I shall go and see her too. I will go by this path, and you by that path, and we will see who gets there first.'

The Wolf set off running with all his might by the shorter

road, and the little girl continued on her way by the longer road. As she went she amused herself by gathering nuts, running after the butterflies, and making nosegays of the wild flowers which she found.

'Making nosegays of the wild flowers'

The Wolf was not long in reaching the grandmother's house.

He knocked. *Toc Toc.*

'Who is there?'

'It is your little daughter, Red Riding Hood,' said the

Wolf, disguising his voice, 'and I bring you a cake and a little pot of butter as a present from my mother.'

The worthy grandmother was in bed, not being very well, and cried out to him:

'Pull out the peg and the latch will fall.'

The Wolf drew out the peg and the door flew open. Then he sprang upon the poor old lady and ate her up in less than no time, for he had been more than three days without food.

After that he shut the door, lay down in the grandmother's bed, and waited for Little Red Riding Hood.

Presently she came and knocked. *Toc Toc.*

'Who is there?'

Now Little Red Riding Hood on hearing the Wolf's gruff voice was at first frightened, but thinking that her grandmother had a bad cold, she replied:

'It is your little daughter, Red Riding Hood, and I bring you a cake and a little pot of butter from my mother.'

Softening his voice, the Wolf called out to her:

'Pull out the peg and the latch will fall.'

Little Red Riding Hood drew out the peg and the door flew open.

When he saw her enter, the Wolf hid himself in the bed beneath the counterpane.

'Put the cake and the little pot of butter on the bin,' he said, 'and come up on the bed with me.'

115

Little Red Riding Hood took off her clothes, but when she climbed up on the bed she was astonished to see how her grandmother looked in her nightgown.

'Come up on the bed with me'

'Grandmother dear!' she exclaimed, 'what big arms you have!'

'The better to embrace you, my child!'

'Grandmother dear, what big legs you have!'

'The better to run with, my child!'

'Grandmother dear, what big ears you have!'

116

'The better to hear with, my child!'
'Grandmother dear, what big eyes you have!'
'The better to see with, my child!'
'Grandmother dear, what big teeth you have!'
'The better to eat you with!'
With these words the wicked Wolf leapt upon Little Red Riding Hood and gobbled her up.

BLUE BEARD

ONCE upon a time there was a man who owned splendid town and country houses, gold and silver plate, tapestries and coaches gilt all over. But the poor fellow had a blue beard, and this made him so ugly and frightful that there was not a woman or girl who did not run away at sight of him.

Amongst his neighbours was a lady of high degree who had two surpassingly beautiful daughters. He asked for the hand of one of these in marriage, leaving it to their mother to choose which should be bestowed upon him. Both girls, however, raised objections, and his offer was bandied from one to the other, neither being able to bring herself to accept a man with a blue beard. Another reason for their distaste was the fact that he had already married several wives, and no one knew what had become of them.

In order that they might become better acquainted, Blue Beard invited the two girls, with their mother and three or four of their best friends, to meet a party of young men from the neighbourhood at one of his country houses. Here they spent eight whole days, and throughout

Blue Beard

their stay there was a constant round of picnics, hunting and fishing expeditions, dances, dinners, and luncheons; and they never slept at all, through spending all the night in playing merry pranks upon each other. In short, everything went so gaily that the younger daughter began to think the master of the house had not so very blue a beard after all, and that he was an exceedingly agreeable man. As soon as the party returned to town their marriage took place.

At the end of a month Blue Beard informed his wife that important business obliged him to make a journey into a distant part of the country, which would occupy at least six weeks. He begged her to amuse herself well during his absence, and suggested that she should invite some of her friends and take them, if she liked, to the country. He was particularly anxious that she should enjoy herself thoroughly.

'Here,' he said, 'are the keys of the two large store-rooms, and here is the one that locks up the gold and silver plate which is not in everyday use. This key belongs to the strong-boxes where my gold and silver is kept, this to the caskets containing my jewels; while here you have the master-key which gives admittance to all the apartments. As regards this little key, it is the key of the small room at the end of the long passage on the lower floor. You may open everything, you may go everywhere, but I forbid you to enter this little room. And I forbid you so seriously that if you were indeed to open the door, I should be so angry that I might do anything.'

She promised to follow out these instructions exactly and after embracing her, Blue Beard steps into his coach and is off upon his journey.

Her neighbours and friends did not wait to be invited before coming to call upon the young bride, so great was their eagerness to see the splendours of her house. They had not dared to venture while her husband was there, for his blue beard frightened them. But in less than no time there they were, running in and out of the rooms, the closets, and the wardrobes, each of which was finer than the last. Presently they went upstairs to the storerooms, and there they could not admire enough the profusion and magnificence of the tapestries, beds, sofas, cabinets, tables, and stands. There were mirrors in which they could view themselves from top to toe, some with frames of plate glass, others with frames of silver and gilt lacquer, that were the most superb and beautiful things that had ever been seen. They were loud and persistent in their envy of their friend's good fortune. She, on the other hand, derived little amusement from the sight of all these riches, the reason being that she was impatient to go and inspect the little room on the lower floor.

So overcome with curiosity was she that, without reflecting upon the discourtesy of leaving her guests, she ran down a private staircase, so precipitately that twice or thrice she nearly broke her neck, and so reached the door of the little room. There she paused for a while, thinking of the prohibition which her husband had made, and reflecting that harm might come to her as a result of disobedience. But the temptation was so great that she could not conquer it. Taking the little key, with a trembling hand she opened the door of the room.

'She washed it well'

At first she saw nothing, for the windows were closed, but after a few moments she perceived dimly that the floor was entirely covered with clotted blood, and that in this were reflected the dead bodies of several women that hung along the walls. These were all the wives of Blue Beard, whose throats he had cut, one after another.

She thought to die of terror, and the key of the room, which she had just withdrawn from the lock, fell from her hand.

123

When she had somewhat regained her senses, she picked up the key, closed the door, and went up to her chamber to compose herself a little. But this she could not do, for her nerves were too shaken. Noticing that the key of the little room was stained with blood, she wiped it two or three times. But the blood did not go. She washed it well, and even rubbed it with sand and grit. Always the blood remained. For the key was bewitched, and there was no means of cleaning it completely. When the blood was removed from one side, it reappeared on the other.

Blue Beard returned from his journey that very evening. He had received some letters on the way, he said, from which he learned that the business upon which he had set forth had just been concluded to his satisfaction. His wife did everything she could to make it appear that she was delighted by his speedy return.

On the morrow he demanded the keys. She gave them to him, but with so trembling a hand that he guessed at once what had happened.

'How comes it,' he said to her, 'that the key of the little room is not with the others?'

'I must have left it upstairs upon my table,' she said.

'Do not fail to bring it to me presently,' said Blue Beard.

After several delays the key had to be brought. Blue Beard examined it, and addressed his wife.

'Why is there blood on this key?'

Sister Anne

' "You must die, madam," he said'

'I do not know at all,' replied the poor woman, paler than death.

'You do not know at all?' exclaimed Blue Beard; 'I know well enough. You wanted to enter the little room! Well, madam, enter it you shall – you shall go and take your place among the ladies you have seen there.'

She threw herself at her husband's feet, asking his pardon with tears, and with all the signs of a true repentance for her disobedience. She would have softened a rock, in her beauty and distress, but Blue Beard had a heart harder than any stone.

'You must die, madam,' he said; 'and at once.'

'Since I must die,' she replied, gazing at him with eyes that were wet with tears, 'give me a little time to say my prayers.'

'I give you one quarter of an hour,' replied Blue Beard, 'but not a moment longer.'

When the poor girl was alone, she called her sister to her and said:

'Sister Anne' – for that was her name – 'go up, I implore you, to the top of the tower, and see if my brothers are not approaching. They promised that they would come and visit me today. If you see them, make signs to them to hasten.'

Sister Anne went up to the top of the tower, and the poor unhappy girl cried out to her from time to time:

'Anne, Sister Anne, do you see nothing coming?'

And Sister Anne replied:

'I see nought but dust in the sun and the green grass growing.'

Presently Blue Beard, grasping a great cutlass, cried out at the top of his voice:

'Come down quickly, or I shall come upstairs myself.'

'Oh please, one moment more,' called out his wife.

And at the same moment she cried in a whisper:

'Anne, Sister Anne, do you see nothing coming?'

'I see nought but dust in the sun and the green grass growing.'

'Come down at once, I say,' shouted Blue Beard, 'or I will come upstairs myself.'

'I am coming,' replied his wife.

Then she called:

'Anne, Sister Anne, do you see nothing coming?'

'I see,' replied Sister Anne, 'a great cloud of dust which comes this way.'

'Is it my brothers?'

'Alas, sister, no; it is but a flock of sheep.'

'Do you refuse to come down?' roared Blue Beard.

'One little moment more,' exclaimed his wife.

Once more she cried:

'Anne, Sister Anne, do you see nothing coming?'

'I see,' replied her sister, 'two horsemen who come this way, but they are as yet a long way off. ... Heaven be praised,' she exclaimed a moment later, 'they are my

'Brandishing the cutlass aloft'

brothers. . . . I am signalling to them all I can to hasten.'

Blue Beard let forth so mighty a shout that the whole house shook. The poor wife went down and cast herself at his feet, all dishevelled and in tears.

'That avails you nothing,' said Blue Beard; 'you must die.'

Seizing her by the hair with one hand, and with the other brandishing the cutlass aloft, he made as if to cut off her head.

The poor woman, turning towards him and fixing a dying gaze upon him, begged for a brief moment in which to collect her thoughts.

'No! no!' he cried; 'commend your soul to Heaven.' And raising his arm——

At this very moment there came so loud a knocking at the gate that Blue Beard stopped short. The gate was opened, and two horsemen dashed in, who drew their swords and rode straight at Blue Beard. The latter recognised them as the brothers of his wife – one of them a dragoon, and the other a musketeer – and fled instantly in an effort to escape. But the two brothers were so close upon him that they caught him ere he could gain the first flight of steps. They plunged their swords through his body and left him dead. The poor woman was nearly as dead as her husband, and had not the strength to rise and embrace her brothers.

It was found that Blue Beard had no heirs, and that

consequently his wife became mistress of all his wealth. She devoted a portion to arranging a marriage between her sister Anne and a young gentleman with whom the latter had been for some time in love, while another portion purchased a captain's commission for each of her brothers. The rest formed a dowry for her own marriage with a very worthy man, who banished from her mind all memory of the evil days she had spent with Blue Beard.

CHARLES PERRAULT (1628–1703) was born in Paris. His father was a barrister, so he studied law, but he found work as a civil servant, first in the offices of his brother, Receveur général des finances, and then as Comptroller of the Royal Buildings for Louis XIV. He also wrote verse and became a member of the Académie Française in 1671. As an Academician he was involved in the 1890s in an intense controversy about the merits of modern – as opposed to classical – writers and when in 1694 he published his verse retelling of a traditional tale, 'Donkey-Skin', he was attacked for writing such childish stories. It is not surprising, therefore, that his famous fairy tales, first published as *Histoires ou contes du temps passé avec des moralités* in 1697, carried the name of his son Pierre Darmancour as the author. Since Pierre was probably just nineteen at the time, it is unlikely he could have produced such skilful telling of the eight fairy tales that have remained so universally appealing for nearly three centuries. They are now always attributed to Perrault. The stories first appeared in English in 1729 and have been in print ever since, under different titles, most often as *Mother Goose's Tales*, the words that appear in the frontispiece of the French edition, depicting the storyteller as an old woman with three spellbound children.

WILLIAM HEATH ROBINSON (1872–1944) was the youngest of the three artist sons of a wood engraver. Born in Hornsey Rise, north London, he studied at Islington School of Art and briefly at the Royal Academy Schools. He then had grandiose ideas of earning a living as a landscape painter, but soon abandoned these and, working from his father's studios in the Strand, began to receive illustrating commissions from publishers. His unmistakable, humorous style first showed itself in a story for children that he both wrote and illustrated, *Uncle Lubin*, published in 1902. He went on to develop this talent in comic cartoons for the *Strand* magazine and other periodicals, devising in his drawings the weird contraptions that later gave his name to the English language for any mechanical device 'absurdly complicated in design and having a simple function'.

By the time his illustrations for the Perrault stories appeared in 1921, he was famous as a comic artist. The translator of the stories, A. E. Johnson, had been his friend and agent since 1903 and was a great help to him both in finding work and negotiating terms with publishers.

William Heath Robinson was a shy and modest man, of whom his son Oliver wrote: 'Fame meant nothing to him, except at one stage. That was when it was widely put about that he was kept under restraint most of the time but, as a concession, allowed out once a week to sell his drawings. That, he felt, was really going too far ...'

TITLES IN
EVERYMAN'S LIBRARY CHILDREN'S
CLASSICS

AESOP *Fables*
Illustrated by Stephen Gooden

Aladdin and other Tales from the Arabian Nights
Illustrated by W. Heath Robinson and others

LOUISA M. ALCOTT *Little Women*
Illustrated by M. E. Gray

Little Men
Illustrated by Frank Merrill

HANS CHRISTIAN ANDERSEN *Fairy Tales*
Illustrated by W. Heath Robinson

GILLIAN AVERY *The Everyman Book of
Poetry for Children*
Illustrated by Thomas Bewick

Russian Fairy Tales
Illustrated by Ivan Bilibin

J. M. BARRIE *Peter Pan*
Illustrated by F. D. Bedford

L. FRANK BAUM *The Wonderful Wizard of Oz*
Illustrated by W. W. Denslow

ROBERT BROWNING *The Pied Piper of Hamelin*
Illustrated by Kate Greenaway

LEWIS CARROLL *Alice's Adventures in Wonderland
and Through the Looking Glass*
Illustrated by John Tenniel

ROALD DAHL *The BFG*
Illustrated by Quentin Blake

DANIEL DEFOE *Robinson Crusoe*
Illustrated by W. J. Linton and others

CHARLES DICKENS *A Christmas Carol*
Illustrated by Arthur Rackham

SIR ARTHUR CONAN DOYLE *Sherlock Holmes*
Illustrated by Sidney Paget

C. S. EVANS *Cinderella*
The Sleeping Beauty
Illustrated by Arthur Rackham

OLIVER GOLDSMITH, WILLIAM COWPER and OTHERS
Ride a-Cock-Horse and other
Rhymes and Stories
Illustrated by Randolph Caldecott

KENNETH GRAHAME *The Wind in the Willows*
Illustrated by Arthur Rackham

THE BROTHERS GRIMM *Fairy Tales*
Illustrated by Arthur Rackham

NATHANIEL HAWTHORNE *A Wonder-Book*
Illustrated by Arthur Rackham

FRANCES HODGSON BURNETT *The Secret Garden*
Illustrated by Charles Robinson

Little Lord Fauntleroy
Illustrated by C. E. Brock

JOSEPH JACOBS *English Fairy Tales*
Illustrated by John Batten

WALTER JERROLD *Mother Goose's Nursery Rhymes*
Illustrated by Charles Robinson

RUDYARD KIPLING *The Jungle Book*
Illustrated by Kurt Wiese

Just So Stories
Illustrated by the Author

Just So Stories
Illustrated by the Author

ROGER LANCELYN GREEN *The Adventures of Robin Hood*
Illustrated by Walter Crane

King Arthur and his Knights
of the Round Table
Illustrated by Aubrey Beardsley

EDWARD LEAR *A Book of Nonsense*
Illustrated by the Author

GEORGE MACDONALD *The Princess and the Goblin*
Illustrated by Arthur Hughes

L. M. MONTGOMERY *Anne of Green Gables*
Illustrated by Sybil Tawse

E. NESBIT *The Railway Children*
Illustrated by C. E. Brock

CHARLES PERRAULT *Little Red*
Riding Hood and other Stories
Illustrated by W. Heath Robinson

ANNA SEWELL *Black Beauty*
Illustrated by Lucy Kemp-Welch

ROBERT LOUIS STEVENSON *A Child's Garden of Verses*
Illustrated by Charles Robinson

Kidnapped
Illustrated by Rowland Hilder

Treasure Island
Illustrated by Mervyn Peake

JEAN WEBSTER *Daddy-Long-Legs*
Illustrated by the Author

OSCAR WILDE *The Happy Prince and*
other Tales
Illustrated by Charles Robinson

JOHANN WYSS *The Swiss Family Robinson*
Illustrated by Louis Rhead